WANING GIBBOUS

Waning Gibbous

Phases

ELLE C

Elle C Writing

Contents

To the ones who will suffer the most
from human carelessness.

2086

The essence of the storm from the night before lingered in the air. The moisture mixed with my skin's sweat was sticky to the touch as I walked around my neighborhood. Before leaving the house, I took a couple of rips off my bong to help calm my thoughts.

With my air pods in and the music cranked loud, my stroll was peaceful. I could hear the chirps of crickets and buzzing of the mosquitos as the sun dipped lower beneath the horizon. It was still light enough that the streetlights hadn't turned on, but I could tell they would soon.

As I walked down my driveway and onto the street, I turned towards the setting sun so that I wouldn't miss the changing colors of the sky – orange and pink mixed with bits of light blue and misty white from the clouds. My thoughts began drifting to the day I had, recalling my frustration with a life where I felt stuck. I knew working a Monday through Friday, 9:00 am to 5:00 pm job was too mundane for me, but what else was there?

Since the weed kicked in, my anger was minimal.

Thoughts of a better future took the place of any irritation within me.

Before long, I was day-dreaming.

Images flashed before my eyes of a life away from this hell hole. Although I love the smell of the aftermath of a rainstorm, the storm itself prevents me from enjoying nature. Not that water is obstructive to life itself; over the last few years, the Midwest had seen its worst rainfall. It's common for our spring season to experience heavy rain, but towards the beginning of the summer and into the middle, we had storm after storm, week after week. I'm fortunate enough to live on high ground – no flooding at my house yet – but I was tired of all the rain we've experienced.

While the day-dreaming continued, it was almost as if I could *feel* a change coming. Something was telling me it was time to let go and change my path. But how? Move to a warmer climate? The Midwest is warm enough, but I want more peace, more sun. Maybe sunny California or soaking up the ocean waves on the beaches of Florida. The weather there is significantly warmer and dryer, but I prefer that to the moisture.

Besides, my skin is sun-kissed, and to feel the heat for more than just a couple months of the year – that was my dream. The only caveat would be dealing with humidity. If I moved to Florida, my wavy hair would just be frizz. The idea seemed worth it, though.

As I approached the top of my street, more images danced in my head, showing me a world only dreams can create – a world without war; a world without hate; a world where nature lived in near-perfect harmony. Let's face it; the predator chasing prey pattern will never extinguish. But can you imagine living with animals? Not necessarily back to the stone ages, a time where cave dwellers covered from head to toe in hair and knuckles calloused from the planet had roamed the earth. But to live among the animals in peace. Where predators hunt their prey for food, and we stop the unnecessary game hunting. You'd think in the year 2086 it would be banned by now. We're almost to the 22nd century, and yet humans are still vile.

Something needs to change; something must change, and still, I can *feel* it. But what?

The sun was out of view, leaving a trail of colors behind, which persuaded the streetlights to awaken. Even though the clouds nearly covered the sky, the stars began shining through, indicating nightfall. The moon was hiding still – too early yet – so without it, darkness was thicker, and there was a faint smell of another storm brewing – wonderful.

If you could hold off until I finish my walk, that would be fantastic. I thought.

I enjoy these evening strolls. They help calm me down before I get ready for bed. Like I said, being with nature is where I feel most at peace – animals just want to survive. They're not intelligent enough to start a war with one another. When it gets dark, the owls begin hooting while the frogs croak. Nature is the only sound I need in my life.

As if to bring me back to reality, I heard tires screeching on the pavement when I rounded the corner of a street that cut my neighborhood in half. The sound alone made my heart stop; the sight sent shivers down my spine.

I pulled the right air pod from my ear to pause my music and watched as a dark, windowless van came tearing down the road cutting off my path. As I froze, I half expected men to jump out and take me with them to some god-awful dungeon to do goodness knows what to me, but the van stopped, and no one jumped out.

Before my brain communicated with my body to run like hell, the driver's side door slowly opened.

"It's time," said a strange-looking man.

He looked human, but my senses were telling me he was not human. His eyes had a bright yellow hue and almost looked cat-like? I shook my head to help my eyes focus, but all that did was help me see more of his unusual features. His hair didn't stick out to me – it was black, nothing special – and it had a goth vibe, you know, that *I hate the world, love the dark side of life* trend from the 1990s? That's where my mind went when I looked at this guy. There was also a streak of white down the side that seemed familiar, and it was long enough that it covered his ears, mostly. Everything else about him may have seemed human, but those ears were a dead giveaway. They looked just like my cat's ears, literally, a spitting image of the ears that were on my cat. Not only were they shaped like a cat's, but they had little hairs that stuck up at the tips – the pointed tips – with flecks of white on the outside, and light pink on the inside.

What the fuck is going on?

"Wh-what? Wh-who are you?" I finally stuttered.

"We don't have time to explain, Eve. You have to come with us," the man replied.

How does he know my name?

After he replied, the passenger door opened, and I heard the sliding of the side door as well. Two more men stepped out, just as strange as the first man.

"Oli, what's taking so long?" said the man who exited the van through the passenger door. He had ginger hair that was kind of long and puffy. He moved his hair behind his ears as if to reveal their similar cat-like appearance. And his voice was deep and powerful like a bass guitar.

"We're going to be late. Eve, it's nice to see you again," said the third man in a chipper voice and a smile. His features were different than the other two – less subtle. His hair was bright blue with a hint of yellow – normal enough – but the tail behind him...

Who are these people?

"Will someone please tell me what the fuck is going on?!" I yelled. There were too many faces I didn't recognize with features I did; an explanation is required right about now.

"Look, Eve, we don't have time to explain. Literally,

the longer we stand here, the less time we have. You see how the sun is almost out of sight?" said the first man – Oli, I guess. I looked towards the sky and noticed what he meant; the stars were twinkling much brighter. But why is that important?

"Yeah, so? What does the sun going down have to do with anything? It's nighttime; that's kind of how it works," I said while rolling my eyes at this delusional...person?

"Oli, explain it on our way there! It's too late now," the blue-haired man with the tail whined. He was growing impatient.

"Eve, please? I promise we're not here to hurt you; we're here to help you. Here, take my gun."

Oli handed me his handgun that he pulled out from a secret holster beneath his jacket. I hesitated but decided it was the better option – me holding onto the exploding weapon instead of this stranger I just met. But if he's so dangerous, why would he allow me to keep possession of his gun? I grabbed it quickly before I could change my mind and checked to make sure it was loaded. I know better than to allow myself to make assumptions, and while I shouldn't trust these men because they tell me to, my gut is telling me everything will be fine; there's something familiar about them in a not creepy way.

"Good. Now, will you please get in the van so we can get a move on?" Oli asked, gesturing towards the passenger door.

Without a verbal response, I got in the van seated

passenger to this man named Oli with cat-like features.

What have I gotten myself into?

Oli drove – quickly – through my neighborhood and out onto the main road. He waited until we were a good ten minutes from my neighborhood before explaining what the fuck I was doing in a van filled with strange-looking men.

"Alright, first, my name is Oliver, and these two are Felix and Pepper," Oliver said as he pointed to Felix, who was the ginger-haired man, and Pepper, who has that tail. Why do these names sound so familiar?

"You're probably wondering why our names sound familiar," Felix began, as if he read my mind, "It's because they are familiar."

"Right! You know us, Eve! And we know you!" shouted Pepper.

"For crying out loud, Pep, if you don't calm your shit, I'm gonna bite a finger off," said Felix while he rubbed his face in the palms of his hands.

"Wow, ok, so, still fucking confused. Why do your names sound familiar, but your faces don't? Who are you guys?!"

They all looked at each other before Oliver decided to respond.

"We're pets – animals. I'm yours to be specific."

What. The. Fuck. I knew something seemed familiar!

My mouth fell to the floor of the van as I tried to process what Oliver just said. Pets? My Oli? My Oli, woli, baby boy? Someone must've laced my weed because I am tripping on some hardcore shit right now.

"Close your mouth before I have to swat a fly away," said Oliver, rolling his eyes.

After looking at him a little longer, I started to see more similarities. Yes, he has cat-like ears that, at first glance, I thought were fake and apart of some weird new fashion trend. Now that I'm looking at them more intently, I can see them moving – on their own – independently from each other. The black hair with the streak of white made more sense; it's the same coloring as my Oli's fur, my black cat.

I shook my head to adjust my eyes again and looked at his. The bright yellow hue had flecks of green and brown; the pupils were vertical and thin, indicating that he was agitated about something. The last thing I looked at was his face. Oli has a very prominent white spot under his left eye. It's how I could always tell him apart from another black cat – well, aside from the random white streak he has. That was still a dead giveaway. It was like he knew I was looking for it because he turned his head in my direction as we slowed to a stop at an intersection.

Yep – that's my Oli. But, a human? Cats can shapeshift?!

"What. The. Fuck," I said, completely and utterly confused. I am tripping – tripping balls.

Oliver sighed before responding.

"I truly hoped we would stop this from happening

to spare you from this turmoil we are now facing. Unfortunately, as the Prophecy predicts, here we are."

"Prophecy? Turmoil? Oli – Oliver – you're being cryptic. I need more than that. I took two huge bong rips before I went for my walk. For all I know, this is just some weird dream I'm having while passed out in the street of my neighborhood. In all my thirty – well, almost thirty – years of being alive, I have never tripped so damn hard before."

The three of them exchanged looks of exasperation again before Felix decided to chime in.

"Would you care to explain, or shall I?" he asked, speaking to Oliver.

Oliver rubbed his face with one hand before sighing again.

"Alright, I can explain everything one of two ways, the hard way, or the easy way," Oliver said.

"Obviously, the easy way. Regardless of how you try to explain this, I'm not going to believe you until I know I've come down from my high," he rolled his eyes at me after that comment.

Before Oliver began explaining, he pulled into the parking lot of a restaurant. According to him, they didn't have time to explain this bullshit to me when we were in my neighborhood, but sure, let's stop for food and have a chat.

"I know what you're thinking," Felix started, "and no, this isn't just a stop for food and chat type of deal. This is our hideout; what better place than a restaurant, right?" He smiled as if he was proud of having the foresight to have a meeting place near food – not that he was wrong.

Oliver led us into the restaurant and towards the back through a secret door. The most cliché part of it was that you needed a password to enter.

When we walked inside, my eyes were indeed deceiving me. There was no way I was staring at a man who had wings like a bird or a woman with a large mare tail. Did that guy just blink sideways at me? Holy fuck, this is a bad trip. It's been a while since I smoked weed laced with acid – fuck me.

Felix found a booth near the back that had more privacy. This time, Pepper chimed into the conversation.

"So, Eve, are you sure you're ready to hear the Prophecy? It's a lot to take in—"

"She doesn't have time to be ready," Oliver interrupted. "Tonight is the night, and the only way to prepare her is to lay it all out."

"Uh, you can stop talking like I'm not sitting right next to you."

Oliver sighed again.

"Alright, the truth is, you're not human."

"What do you mean, I'm not human? Don't I look human to you? I don't have random, animalistic features like you three and, well, the rest of this group of, um, creatures. Why do you think I'm not human?"

"If I'm going to explain, you have to let me tell you everything without interruptions. Agreed? Otherwise, it'll take all night or days, and we only have hours,"

Oliver stated, looking at his watch, "eleven to be exact." I nodded in agreement and took a drink of water that Felix got for me and just listened while Oli – Oliver – explained.

"Almost thirty years ago, the last red wolf was born, and she was beautiful. The most beautiful red wolf that anyone had seen in decades. The flecks of red on her ears danced across her fur, mixing with the brown and gray to create the most magnificent, smoky wood coloring anyone had ever seen. Before she was born, her father was killed in a tragic accident. Unfortunately, her mother died in childbirth.."

Pepper and Felix exchanged a despairing look. Something told me I signed up for something big, something cliché ending with me saving the day, and the entire world is at peace, and I am not on board.

"On the night that the last red wolf was born, the Prophecy had begun, which included protecting her from the world until she was ready. A few animals nearby – myself included – gave you a concoction given to us by a healer that would suppress your animal instincts for as long as your parents administered it. To be sure this would continue, we found a couple who was desperate to have a family of their own and told them everything. They agreed to take you in, kept giving you the suppressant, but now we need your powers."

"My what? What did you explain to them? My parents aren't my real parents? I'm a fucking wolf?!"

"Oli, I told you this was crazy. She's never going to

believe in time; this was a waste." Pepper said with a look of sadness in his eyes. The kind of sadness you see in your pet's eyes when you leave them for the day. Fuck me; I have to hear them out now.

"Alright," I sighed, "you win. So, I'm this red wolf, right?" They nodded. "And I'm supposed to help save the world?"

"Well, not the world," Oliver began, "but the Midwest, specifically."

"Why just the Midwest? What is happening to the Midwest that is so life-threatening? We haven't had a war on our soil since 2020." They all started nodding and looked upset with the memories of that dreadful year.

"The Flood," Felix whispered.

"*The* Flood? Why is it *the* flood?"

"Because this flood will sink the Midwest," said Pepper. All I could do was stare and wonder how a flood so massive would sink the entire Midwest.

You're probably wondering how only the Midwest would be affected and not the rest of the country. Well, in 2050, there was an event that occurred called The Division of the Regions. It had seemed as though none of the Regions of the United States could agree on politics – typical. The one thing they did agree on was to separate themselves physically from each other. Every Region built massive motes and bridges between themselves. They chipped off edges of their states to accomplish this. It had only taken five years to complete, but there has never been such a massive divide in this country's history. Even though we are divided, we still refer to ourselves as the United States. I think some of us are holding on to hope that we'll come together again one day.

We must.

"So, what is causing this massive flood that is only targeting the Midwest?"

Oliver cleared his throat before responding, "You remember that one thing that scientists have warned humans would be a problem if they didn't do something about it now, well, at this point, almost 100 years ago?"

"Um, no, that was extremely vague. There are a million things scientists tell us to do that humans ignore," I said, rolling my eyes in the process.

"Climate Change; Global Heating; Global Warming; take your pick. Either way, the chemicals that we've failed to regulate and minimize are why there has been more rain over the last few years than is normal. The amount of greenhouse gases that have been released into the atmosphere has finally taken full effect. The ozone is too moist, too warm, from all those gases. The moisture has now collected to the point of releasing a massive amount of rain."

All I could do was stare at him with mouth wide open and eyes drying from the lack of blinking. Is he serious? I mean, I knew we were fucking ourselves over by not listening to scientists and nearly killing our planet, but this bullshit has finally caught up to us? I honestly did not think I would be alive to witness the collapse of our environment.

"Wow, um, ok, so this is really happening. We've really fucked ourselves on this, haven't we? But still, how are my powers that have been suppressed for almost thirty years, supposed to help now? And how am I supposed to know how to use them without any training?" Oliver looked at me with weary eyes.

"Right," Oliver began, "there is the part about revealing your powers. That one is going to be a little tricky, but I have faith. I know you, Eve, you can do this." Oliver patted me on the shoulder to show he had faith in my abilities. My pet cat was a human sitting next to me and telling me I'm actually a red wolf whose destiny is to save the Midwest from the flood; that's not weird at all.

"So, what now?" I asked. Oliver looked at Felix as if it was his turn to explain what the next step was.

"We meet with the healer: The Queen Bee," Felix said with a very somber tone.

"The Queen Bee? Like, literally a bee, or is she a human too?"

"Well, she's a bee, but she's a shifter, and she will be in her human form. Ah, here she is now."

As I turned to look towards the entrance to the backroom, in walked this beautiful, hourglass figure of a woman. Her hair was yellow and black, which only looked cheesy because I knew the truth. Otherwise, I would have envied the yellow undertone with black on top and probably thought about getting the same hairstyle. Her clothes were flawless too: black body-con dress with a deep v front, showing off her massive tits, and yellow accents along the seams. She was wearing stiletto heels with red bottoms that looked impossible to walk in, but she seemed to glide through the room. Don't even get me started on her flawless makeup: vibrant red lips, yellow eyes framed with black eyeliner so sharp, you'd swear it could cut glass.

"Whoa," I said, jaw to the floor and eyes wide as ever.

"Close your mouth, dear, you're letting the flies enter," she said. Fuck me – her voice was as flawless as her looks.

"We're running out of time, Guinevere," started Oliver. Of course, her name is Guinevere. The Queen bee? Queen Guinevere? Fuuuck. "Can you restore Eve's memories and powers so we can stop the end of the world for the Midwest?"

"Why would I want to do that? She's so pretty in human form. There's no telling what her temper will be like as a wolf."

"That's not your call to make, Guin. Please, it's time," this time, Felix piped up.

"Fine, have it your way. But I'm warning you; the side effects from that suppressant are not pleasant. You'll want me to reverse this in private, and somewhere relatively remote."

Why does it feel like I'm about to go through the worst transformation of my life that may or may not end in me dying? I never asked for any of this. I just want to go back to my everyday life – my human only life – or do I?

The men – animals? Whatever – led us out back where there was a wooded area with a clearing. My stomach began knotting at the idea of shifting into an animal and the potential of dying from it. I know I said it would be cool to be at peace with the animals, but becoming one was not what I thought that meant.

"Stand right in the middle, beautiful," said Guinevere. Wow, her voice is like velvet.

"Front and center for all of us to witness! Oh, yay!" Pepper was way too excited. What animal is he?

"Shut up, tweety!" yelled Felix.

Ah, that makes sense.

Pepper...where have I heard that name before?

"Are you ready?" Guinevere asked.

"I mean, do I have a choice?"

"Nope, not enough time," Oliver replied. "We've already wasted an hour; let's go, Guin."

"You can't rush perfection, Oliver," she purred.

Guinevere grabbed a bag that I swear she didn't have when she arrived and set down some beakers – potions, I assumed. As if I picked up an old storybook with images of the witch's brew and her bottles of potions, she pulled out various beakers in all shapes, sizes, and colors: pink, green, blue, and yellow. Most of them had a round bottom and skinny neck; some shaped like the one you'd find in a historical science classroom where students did physical experiments instead of using the machines we have today. I can only imagine how tedious all that used to be; I guess I'm about to find out.

The last thing she grabbed from the bag was a mat with inscriptions. None of them had familiar letters, and it was a language I didn't recognize. Maybe Russian? Regardless, whatever was about to happen was big, and I wasn't entirely sure I was ready for it.

I was a little disappointed when Guinevere set a large bowl in front of the mat instead of a cauldron. But I guess not everything you read in stories is right about witches, or I guess in her case, healers. Is there a difference?

She started adding the liquids in a peculiar order: first pink, then green, then pink again, then yellow, more pink potion, and finally blue. After she added the blue liquid, she sat cross-legged with her eyes closed and hands together in front of her torso, clasped at the fingers so that one hand was on top of the other. Imagine the yin and yang symbol but with your hands.

Guinevere cleared her throat, indicating she was about to begin. "This spell does not use words, for words are a human's weapon. Instead, it uses the energy that is within all living beings. Some of us have stronger energy than others; that is why I am a healer." Her voice is so soothing I could fall asleep just listening to her talk.

She closed her eyes and started making an ohm sound as if she was meditating. The bowl responded by slowly rising from the ground. When it was nearly eye level with me, I noticed that it was more than just a bowl; it was a beehive – go figure. As it reached its peak elevation, a swarm of bees came buzzing out. The bees' colors were the same as the potions poured into the hive; some green, some yellow, but most of them were pink. Then they started circling me.

Oh, fuck no! I am not about to get stung by a swarm of bees! I don't care if they're harmless – it hurts!

"You're joking, right?!" I yelled, mostly because the swarm of bees was making it hard to hear anything else, and Guinevere's ohm sounds were louder as well.

"Be still, child. They are not all going to sting you," she assured me. "At least, not all at once." With that, she smirked an evil smirk. Why am I trusting this woman – bee – that I just met?

"It's alright, Eve," Oliver started, "you'll be fine. Your skin is tougher than you think."

Strangely enough, Oliver was right. The bees began stinging me in the order that Guinevere poured the different colored potions. First, a chunk of the pink ones covered my arms and legs and stung me; I didn't feel any of them. Then, all the green ones covered my neck. There wasn't a lot, but even still, I felt nothing. The next group of pink ones repeated the process on my feet and hands. Those tingled a little but not in a painful way. Finally, the remaining colors swarmed the rest of my body. The pink covered my head, but just my head; Yellow went for my torso, and blue finished by covering my face. The ones on my face hit a nerve.

There was a hint of pain, but it was brief and manageable.

The whole process felt like it lasted an hour, but it had only been a couple of moments when all was said and done. The weird part was that everyone was staring at me like I was about to combust spontaneously.

"Am I supposed to feel diff—"

Suddenly, I couldn't speak. It felt like my tongue swelled my mouth shut, but I could still breathe in and out through my mouth and nose. My vision blurred slightly until everything went completely black. Panic sunk in while I patted at my face trying to see my hands, but instead of feeling my skin, I felt fur. Every attempt I made at speaking was useless. My heart was pounding in my chest, and the heat was rising within me. My breathing became more profound, heavier, and I could hear that it sounded different too. It sounded primal.

As if I had been through the worst of it, my bones reminded me that I was only part of the way through what I could assume was my first ever shift. It started in my legs around the calves; I could feel them lengthening, stretching, tearing from their human shapes. The pain was excruciating, but the only sound I could make was a whimper. The same sensation happened in my arms, only quicker, and my fingers and toes followed suit shortly after. All I wanted was to be able to see. I want to see what is happening to my body.

And then it happened.

My ass felt like someone shoved their hand inside,

up to the middle of my back, latched onto my spine and just pulled. The pulling sensation lasted for what felt like days, weeks, years. But of course, you can't be a wolf without a fluffy tail. I tried to reach back to touch it but moving my right arm towards my rear end was not possible in this form without sending me face planting on the ground. My audience must be enjoying the show I'm putting on for them this evening.

After a few moments, I realized the transformation was complete, but I still couldn't see.

"Eve, open your eyes," Oliver whispered.

Did I have my eyes closed this whole time?

I listened, and when I did, I could tell I was in a different form just by looking at the people – er, animals – who brought me here. My wolf form was taller than I anticipated, so the guys were nearly eye level with me. After I blinked a few times to help clear away my tears, the world revealed its beauty.

My senses heightened significantly. I could hear a rushing river that I knew for a fact was at least a mile or more away. There were creatures in the woods stomping on twigs as if they were safe from predators – foolishness. The smell of Oliver and Felix was slightly repulsive. It made me shake my head to get the scent out, but it was no use. Pepper smelled like dinner. He's your companion, Eve, not food.

Then I saw it: the moon. Before I had a second to process anything, my legs and arms decided to start running, running towards the moon, or at least towards a clearing so I could get a better view. In my heart of hearts, I knew I was meant to do this. The closer I was to an open area, the more my bones ached with excitement and anticipation.

Then I felt it.

The pull from the moon's lunar surface felt like an imaginary string tugging at my heart. My body started convulsing from my chest, and before my brain could register what was happening –

"Hooooooo!"

My heart was singing while my voice echoed through the forest. It was a sensation that I had never felt before, but it felt fantastic; it felt right.

"HoooOOOO!"

"Glad to have you back, Eve," Oliver said as he and the rest of the group stepped out of the thick of the trees. They were still in their human form, but I could see even more of their animalistic features; smell their different scents.

I began panting from the running I did. My body wasn't used to running in general but as a wolf? I'm surprised I'm still standing.

"Well," Guinevere began, "now that we've got that out of the way, we need to talk about your powers."

"Can't she enjoy being a wolf just a little longer?" This time, Pepper was pleading my case, a case I didn't even realize needed pleading. But he was right, I enjoyed being a wolf, and I knew that if we need to discuss my powers, I needed to transform back into a human so I could talk. But how the fuck am I supposed to do that?

"Don't worry, Eve," Guinevere said, "transforming will be easy now. All you have to do is think *really* hard about being a human. Soon it'll be natural and effortless. This first one will be the tricky one."

Right, just think really hard about being a human. The problem is, I don't want to be a human. I feel so strong, so powerful in this form. As a human, I'm weak and pathetic. Being a wolf felt natural, and now that I'm here, everything in my life started to make sense. I began whimpering when Oliver approached me.

"Eve, we all know how much more enjoyable it is to be an animal, but we need you to change back so we can get you used to your magic. You can use it in both human and wolf form, but the only way to understand it is by practicing as a human." I looked at him with sad puppy-dog eyes and tilted my head to the side, hoping he would change his mind. "Nice try, but that dog pout doesn't work on cats. Shift now before I scratch your nose."

Wow, he went from pleasant to nasty real quick. I guess I'm not surprised since he's a cat. I could just run away and avoid this whole situation, but my gut told me that if I didn't comply and save the Midwest, I'd be miserable for the rest of my life. I started thinking about my family – while estranged, they're still my family – specifically my mom. She and I had a falling out a couple of years back, and we never made up. Regardless, I would walk through hellfire to make sure she was safe.

My body started feeling weird again. I could feel

the bones in my arms and legs beginning to shrink back to their puny human form along with my muscles. My face started itching as my elongated muzzle retracted back into a human mouth. My senses were definitely back to normal; I could hardly tell two cats, and a bird was in my presence.

Why is being a human so dull?

"Welcome back, Eve," Pepper said with a grin. Oliver patted me on the back and escorted me back to the group. Guinevere gestured for all of us to sit down – except me – and began explaining how to use my powers.

"First, your powers are extraordinary and exactly what we need to stop the flood destined for the Midwest. It's going to sound strange, but you can manipulate objects with your mind."

I think being a wolf for that brief moment made me forget how to hear because it sounded like she just said I could manipulate shit...with my mind? I must have been gawking because Guinevere rolled her eyes at me.

"Yes, you can manipulate shit with your mind. Didn't you boys tell her I can read minds, too?"

"Y–," I stuttered. Talking seemed more challenging now. "You can read minds?!"

"Yes, Eve," Felix chimed in, "she's a healer; all healers can read minds." He said it as though it was common knowledge.

Thanks, asshole, but all this shit is new to me.

Guinevere smiled.

"Felix," Oliver began, "she just found out she was *the* red wolf. What makes you think any of this was information she knew?"

"Ok, boys, enough. We have an entire chunk of the United States to save. You can save your bickering for after." Guinevere walked towards me – no, glided – and grabbed both of my hands. "This will be easy; easier than shifting back and forth between your human and wolf form for the first time. Something tells me you know how to do this already."

She was right. Ever since I was a kid, I knew I was different, but I didn't understand why. Not that I could pull *Matilda* type shit, but it was close enough to send bullies running. There was one time I made a snake slither across the feet of Armand Goldschmidt. He screamed like a little girl, but he deserved it. He told me I was adopted, and my parents never loved me. Fucking dick.

Look at me now, Armand.

"So, what do I do? I mean, I've kinda done it before, but like, do I think about it, imagine it, what's the deal here?"

"You feel it."

What.

"Yes, you feel it."

"Is that all I get? No, *you feel it in your bones,* or *imagine the object doing what you want?*"

"Just feel it." Guinevere looked annoyed now, but can you blame me? I've never honed in on these skills before; I feel like a baby.

"You've got this, Eve!" shouted Pepper. Thanks for the moral support, buddy.

Alright, Eve, feel it, just feel it. Feel what? What do I want to manipulate?

"Start small," Guinevere said, "Throw that rock."

She pointed at a rock right in front of me. *That's child's play*, I thought. *I can do better than that.* When I looked up, I saw a boulder.

Oh, yeah, kick it into gear, Eve. Show them you can do this!

Oliver must have sensed that I was challenging Guinevere because he shifted his feet as if he would attempt to stop me, but didn't. Guinevere was right; I could feel the energy in the boulder resonate through the earth. It shook me from the inside ever so slightly – like a tremor in the ground on the outskirts of an earthquake. Even though the boulder was an inanimate object, the energy it gave off felt alive, alive enough to manipulate.

I closed my eyes – for dramatic effect – and imagined the boulder levitating above the ground. When I opened my eyes, the boulder was levitating above the ground. I smirked and looked towards the group as I watched their faces change from skepticism to belief. I knew I could do it; well, I thought maybe it was possible.

"You did it, Eve!" shouted Pepper.

"Good job, kid," said Felix with an agreeable nod.

"I knew you had it in you," Oliver smiled.

"That's not good enough," Guinevere said, sternly.

Well, damn, bitch. It was the first time I've knowingly used my powers. A little praise would be excellent.

"Harsh much, Guin?" said Oliver.

"Throw it," Guinevere said.

Fine – I'll throw the damn boulder. I closed my eyes again and repeated the feeling of lifting the boulder but focused my energy towards throwing it into the woods. The boulder's energy was weaker this time, so I opened my eyes slightly to see if anything happened – nothing. Closing my eyes again and repeating the energy feeling thing, but with even more focus, it felt like my body would burst. I realized I was holding my breath and starting panting as I opened my eyes only to find nothing happened; the boulder fell with a loud crash.

"What the fuck?!" I screamed, extremely irritated, "I did the same thing I did when I lifted it. Why isn't it moving?" I looked to the group for some encouragement, but they all looked disappointed with me now – almost scared.

"It's not the same feeling for every manipulation," Guinevere said, rolling her eyes in the process.

"So, what feeling is it then?"

"Only the red wolf knows."

Wow, cryptic, much?

Eve, you've got this. Focus on what it would feel like if someone threw you. I bet that's the key, feeling the sensation you're attempting to manipulate. Lifting was easy – my dad lifted me all the time – throwing is different. I can only assume being thrown would feel like you're flying with the wind rushing through your hair and across your skin. With that in mind, I closed my eyes again – I'm telling you, it helps with the concentration – and imagined what the boulder would feel as it is being thrown.

The wind picked up as soon as my eyelids fell shut, and my hair and clothes started flapping with the breeze. My entire body was vibrating even more than before, and this time I knew it was working. I'm slightly superstitious, so I kept my eyes closed to prevent any bad juju.

I heard a collective *whoa* behind me and smiled – it's working. The next sensation that rippled through me was the force of launching an object with as much effort as possible. The energy moved through my body, starting in my toes and moving through my fingers towards the boulder. I heard the whipping of wind, leaves, and twigs and opened my eyes. The boulder was soaring through the air, deep into the woods.

"Booyah! Did it, bitches!"

"Well done," responded Guinevere in a very *you got lucky* tone. It didn't bother me; I was jumping for joy at this fantastic accomplishment.

"Child's play," I smirked.

"Exactly the problem," Guin replied. "Lifting boulders and throwing them is an amazing accomplishment for someone who has never used their powers before. But to save the Midwest, you will need to muster up all of your energy, because lifting an entire region is going to take every fiber of your being."

"Lifting – the entire Region? I have to lift the Midwest?!"

"How else do you avoid flooding?" Oliver asked as if it was common knowledge that lifting would be the solution to this problem.

"Can't I just move the water?"

"Where are you going to put it?" Felix started, "the sky? The ground? A river or ocean? The only way to avoid floods is by moving up, like towards the sky. Water will continue to flow no matter where it's located, and if it's just moved, you're dooming another region."

I hated it, but Felix was right. I'm an idiot.

Lifting the Midwest makes the most sense, but for how long? Hours? Days? Weeks?

"Minutes." Oh yeah. Guin can read minds.

"That's it? Minutes?"

"Believe it or not, yes. You only need to lift the Midwest for minutes, but you won't begin until you're instructed. We must be precise; our deadline is 6:29 am."

"Why 6:29 am? That seems like a very particular time," I asked.

"Because that's when the sun begins to rise," Guin replied, "and we only have until the start of a new day. That is why your training is accelerated. The Prophecy states that at the start of the last moon cycle before the red wolf's thirtieth birthday, the world will begin to meet its darkest days."

That's why the moon was hidden for the start of my walk. All too often, I've noticed that right after a full moon, the next moon phase – the waning gibbous – doesn't make an appearance right away. It hides, almost like it's waiting for night to fall before it lights up the sky with its beautifully bright glow.

"Alright, I guess that makes sense. But I'm still struggling with where the water will go. If I lift the Midwest, won't it just slide down and target another region? How is *that* going to be prevented?"

"It will be absorbed into the earth around the landmass and drift down the newly formed rivers. They're low enough right now that it won't flood over into other Regions. The issue we face is the inevitable wipe out that the Midwest will experience if we don't stop this tonight." Guin was referring to the rivers that separated the new Division of the Regions. When the Regions built barriers, the rivers widened and deepened. If I don't lift the Midwest, the water will devour the Region and still leave the others untouched.

"What if I can't do it?"

"If we don't try," Pepper chimed in, "we'll never know. But I know you can do this, Eve. I have never seen a newly transformed animal use their powers so quickly before. You have the strength deep in your heart." At that, Pepper walked towards me and patted me on the back. He gave me an optimistic look of hope and belief in my abilities. I know he's the more optimistic one of the group, but something in those dark brown eyes of his told me everything I needed to know – I can do this.

"Alright, I can do this. How much time do we have?"

"About eight more hours," Oliver said, "plenty of time to practice, prepare and get to the location."

Practice: practice makes perfect, right? But a specific location? What the fuck have I gotten myself into?

Guinevere was the leader in my last-minute training session. She was the logical choice given her healing abilities and apparent wisdom that the others seem to lack – except Oliver. He was definitely the leader of the three men, which makes me proud. I need to remember to give him more treats later.

Guin began teaching me how to feel energies deeper to get better control of the object. She said I was a quick learner, and Oliver told her it was from all the yoga and meditating. I'm glad I picked those up; I've never felt more centered or in control of my own body. It's making manipulating objects that much easier.

"Can she try throwing one of us?" Pepper asked, jumping in place.

"Why would that be useful with helping her lift an entire region?" Felix asked, "What, do you think your body amounts to the weight of a region? Pep, she needs to start lifting heavier. That boulder was more than twice your size." Felix couldn't have said it better. Pepper was tiny, and I needed more massive objects to lift.

"We're never going to find something that's even remotely close to the Midwest's weight," Pepper replied, "what makes you think she's going to be ready?" Wow, what happened to happy-go-lucky, optimistic Pepper? I miss that guy.

"She'll be ready," Oliver replied, sternly.

"Thanks, Oli," I said with a smile. It was the first time I called him Oli all night; it was the first time I felt like he was my Oli. He smiled.

Guinevere was looking at me like I was a lost cause. She wasn't helping; all she did was throw things at me and tell me to stop them. I'm not exactly sure how that is supposed to help. She claimed the repetition would strengthen my core – figuratively speaking – and help me focus all of my energy on the Midwest.

"Won't I need to imagine the Region while trying to lift it? I mean, I know the general outline, but I don't want to overshoot or undershoot."

"You're right," Felix replied, "which is why I brought a map."

Oh, good, they came prepared.

"How do we even know this training is work—"

She caught me off guard, but my body knew how to respond before my brain even recognized what was happening. I was facing Oli when my left arm swept behind my back with my palm facing out as if I was telling someone – or something – to stop. That's not all; my right arm was glowing a cool blue and white, almost like the flames of the hottest fire you've ever seen, but I wasn't hot. The ground looked as though a helicopter was flying overhead, with the wind from the blades flattening the grass.

"Eve," When I looked up, Oli was staring at me like a deer in the headlights, and then he had an ear-to-ear grin on his face that sent shivers down my spine.

"She did it! I knew she could do it!" shouted Pepper.

"Well done, Eve," Felix said, almost surprised as if he didn't think I'd manage.

"You've done it!" That was the first time Guinevere had exclaimed anything all evening.

But she had good reason.

I knew why they were all so thrilled to see me glowing like this; this is magic. Guinevere unlocked the real power that I have, which is more than just manipulating objects just by feeling it. This magic that I'm feeling is so powerful; I could use it to do more than just save a region from a flood that would completely sink everything. I could use this to cure diseases, cancer, and viruses; this could help save millions of lives.

The glow around me was still radiating when Oli came over to snap me back to reality.

"You felt it, didn't you?" he asked. I could only nod in reply.

"Now that you know how truly powerful you are, do you think you can handle lifting the Midwest?" Guinevere asked. Again, my only reply was a nod. My abilities dumbfounded me.

Was magic within me this whole time? Like, real, witchy, magic?

"Not witchy, just good 'ole magic." Of course, mind reader.

"Right, well, yes and no. I get that it's there and now it's unlocked, but I'm still not sure how to control it. Like, do I still use my senses, or?"

Felix crossed his arms and rolled his eyes before responding, "Why is it always a dog that has to save the world? Hasn't the universe learned how idiotic they are?"

"Dude, fuck off," replied Oli. I hadn't figured out why Felix hates me so much, but it's getting old.

"Now that you've unlocked your magic," Guinevere thankfully interrupted, "it will come as naturally as talking. You'll just do it because it's engrained in your make."

Why is everything just engrained within me?

"So, what, we're done practicing?"

"Yes, we have completed your training. Everything will be that much easier in your wolf form. Now, we must get in position to prepare for The Flood." Guinevere turned towards the restaurant and gestured for us to follow. She offered to drive since her car was more spacious, and I quote, lacks the creepy stalker vibe. I'm glad I'm not the only one who thought that about the van. Oli said that Pepper picked it out. That makes me worried for his sanity.

I wish I could say Guinevere's means of transportation would be less conspicuous, but it was the exact opposite.

I call it her means of transportation because there was no way this was a car. It looked like a spaceship: bullet-shaped with a pointed front, wings, and an oversized exhaust. But after squinting my eyes and looking a little closer, it was clear as day a stinger from a bee, a giant fucking stinger with the butt still attached. The front was the pointed tip of the stinger with the oversized exhausts as the tail-end. It was a repulsive brown and yellow color with a few dark brown stripes going vertically.

"Are we supposed to get inside...that?" I said, pointing at this monstrosity of a vehicle.

"That, my dear," Guinevere replied, "is my first husband's stinger. He wanted me to remember him, always, and chopped off his lower half as a keepsake. And yes, that is life-size," she smirked and walked towards her husband's stinger – what a weirdo.

"Won't that be suspicious to humans?" I asked because if I saw a giant bee's stinger driving down the highway, I'd question my sanity.

"There's a glimmer over it; to them, it looks like a minivan," her reply had a hint of annoyance. "Now, if you all would please make your way into my vehicle so that we may be going, the rain is going to start soon."

She was right; I could smell the storm approaching. We still had some time, maybe a couple of hours, but it wouldn't be long until the end was here.

The boys climbed in first; Pepper was in the front seat riding passenger to Guin, Oliver climbed in the farthest back row – there were two rows in the back – and Felix climbed into the middle while helping me get situated. Felix shifted when I sat down after my hand accidentally brushed his. It sent a shockwave through my arm and into my chest. I can only imagine he felt something similar because I could see the same confusion when I looked at his gorgeous green eyes. Felix hasn't been my biggest fan through all of this – it's not like I asked to be the red wolf – but the way he's looking at me makes me feel like his attitude towards me was a cover.

Oliver must have felt the tension because he cleared his throat before he began speaking.

"Eve, since you will be lifting the Midwest, we need to get to a place on the outskirts. You won't be able to accomplish your goal if you are in the middle of the Region. Instead, we are going to Wyoming; we're close enough to make it in time. It's about an hour's drive, but I promise it will feel like minutes."

"What's the plan when we get there?" I asked.

"You will get into position," Felix replied, "and Guin will cast a protection spell."

"Why a protection spell?"

"Because if you fail—"

"Felix," Oli interjected, "she won't fail."

"But if she does, we must protect her!"

The passion in Felix's voice made my entire body

shudder. He was panting, and his face had a slight pinkish-red hue appearing – is he embarrassed?

"Felix, we know she must be protected," Oli rested his right hand on Felix's back to console him. "We all saw what happened in that clearing – she can do this. Her magic is back at near full capacity."

"Keyword: near," Felix rolled his eyes.

"Felix," this time, I rested my left hand on Felix's leg. His face turned a brighter red, and I could see sweat beads forming on his forehead. "I've taken in a lot of information this evening; hell, I still can't figure out how I recognize you," his eyes flicked to mine, and the sadness in them made my heart skip a beat, "but I can feel it, down to my core. I know I can do this."

"Eve—"

"I gotta pee!" Pepper interrupted.

When I turned to look at Felix again, everything I needed to know about how I recognized him was written all over his face. Like Oli, Felix has known me for as long as I can remember. But his owner usually refers to him as *ginger shit* or *soulless kitty*. I never knew his real name, and to this day, don't understand how people can own an animal and treat it like garbage. These creatures depend on us – well, I guess they don't entirely – but as far as we know, our pet's only hope for survival is through us, and what are we if we don't treat them well by feeding them, loving them, giving them a warm home?

Felix used to run away and come to my house sometimes. He and Oli would cuddle while I read a book before bed. The only time Felix left Oli's side was when it was bedtime; he would cuddle with me, keeping me warm and purring me to sleep. How it took me so long to recognize him...

"He's a dick anyhow," I said, looking at Felix and squeezing the leg that my hand was still resting on. Felix gave me a weak side smile before reaching his hand to mine and squeezing it back.

"You've got this," he said.

We pulled into the next gas station's parking lot so that Pepper could take his pee break. I took this as an opportunity to stretch my – human – legs and grab a snack. Guinevere said I shouldn't attempt this on an empty stomach.

After exiting the vehicle, I took in the sounds and scents surrounding me. Nothing smelled or sounded the same anymore. Knowing what I do now, it was as if a force reminded me that there was more to nature than what my human senses could show me. The air was crisp, the bugs chirped louder, and my heart sang a different tune.

I could get used to this, I thought, *being a wolf.*

I smiled and continued towards the gas station convenience store. On my way inside, something didn't feel right. It was hard to explain, but I stopped walking, closed my eyes, and breathed in whatever it was.

There was a shift in the air – an unnatural shift. It was subtle, but now that my wolf senses are at near-full capacity, it was like being hit by a train. The air was thicker, more moisture, and the sounds of nature stopped. It was like someone hit the pause button on the music right when you are getting used to the white noise. When I opened my eyes, I was face to face with Oli.

"We're out of time," only, it was me that made the statement. Oli looked at me with wide eyes before he grabbed my arm to pull me towards the stinger mobile. Guin looked at me like she knew what was happening, hopped in the driver seat, and started the vehicle. "Felix, Pep," when I turned to look for them, Felix was running towards us with Pepper on his shoulder, pants around his knees, ass in the air.

"I was mid-stream!"

"There's no time! Can't you feel that?!"

"All I can feel are my balls getting crushed by your shoulder! You have piss on your arm now!" Pepper laughed.

"I'm gonna eat you, bird!" Felix's face was red with what I assumed was embarrassment. I would be embarrassed to have a man's ass in my face with his piss dripping down my arm too.

But now is not the time for fun.

"Hurry," Oli said calmly. He's holding his composure well.

After the boys joined us in the...stinger...Guinevere hit the gas, and we were on our way. Taking the sharp turns a little too quickly; we were in a panic, discussing what was about to happen.

"Eve," Guin began, "as Felix mentioned, I will cast

a protection spell around all of us when you're in position. You'll need us with you in case something doesn't go right. Once the spell is in place, you will need to shift into your wolf form and focus all of your energy on the Midwest's outline. Felix, do you have the map?"

"Right here," Felix replied as he handed it to me. I knew the Midwest – generally speaking – but the map helped me focus on the states. I started from the top and outskirts: North Dakota, South Dakota, Nebraska, Kansas, Missouri, Illinois, Indiana, Ohio, Michigan, Wisconsin, Minnesota, and lastly, Iowa. I repeated the states in my head until I could close my eyes and see them as clear as day.

I didn't realize my hands were shaking until Felix rested his hands on mine. He looked at me, gave a half-smile, and said, "I know you've got this."

"We all do," added Oli. It was hard to believe them.

The car ride seemed like it lasted another half a day. Every second that passed felt like a half-hour. You know those butterflies you get in your stomach when you see your crush? Yeah, that's what was going on with me. By the time we arrived at the location, the sky had started changing colors from a dark midnight blue to a light baby blue. With the sun still hiding, the moon was beginning to turn opaque. I remember when we started this evening, Oli said we had until the sun came up or all hope was lost.

Didn't Guin say we have until—

"6:29 am. Places everyone," Guin announced. We

pulled up to the location and hopped out of the vehicle as fast as we could. "Eve, you'll be standing front and center." She pointed to an invisible spot on the ground that I needed to be. We made it to the planned location – Wyoming – just in time. As I got into position, I looked down at the ground at the divide between the Regions, and my heart started racing.

This is really happening.

"Eve," Felix began, "we're right behind you. Just breathe, concentrate, and focus on that god-forsaken Region," he smiled, patted me on the back, and took a step back to get himself situated.

My heart started pounding harder than ever before. Even harder than one of my distance runs. I thought it would beat right out of my damn chest. My breaths became quicker and shallower, and I knew that I needed to concentrate; I needed to close my eyes.

Before I closed my eyes, I turned to look at the group.

Guinevere: the healer, the Queen Bee.

Pepper: The annoying pet bird who's always upbeat – thankful for him.

Felix: My abusive neighbor's beautiful, fiery orange tabby cat who I've loved since the day I met him.

Oliver: Last, but most certainly not least, my most precious boy. The black panther of a cat who has stood by my side no matter what life has thrown our way.

I gave them all a smile and nod and turned towards the Midwest.

"The protection spell is in place," Guinevere announced. "Deep breaths, concentrate your magic, save the Midwest."

"Right, no big deal," I chuckled nervously.

With that, I turned all my thoughts on the Midwest and the states within: North Dakota, South Dakota, Nebraska, Kansas, Missouri, Illinois, Indiana, Ohio, Michigan, Wisconsin, Minnesota, Iowa. I repeated over and over until I could see their outline. While holding onto the names, I shifted back into wolf form. It was easier this time, and I could tell my magic was more potent than in my human form.

As I took in a deep breath, I felt another shift in the air. This time all the hot air had disappeared, and it was as cold as a fall evening. We're in the middle of summer; that is not normal. The sounds of nature were still nonexistent, which started giving me chills. Nature knows when something is not right.

All was quiet for a moment.

Then the rain came.

The smell of moisture in the air was overpowering, but the rain's sound was nothing I'd ever heard before. It was as if someone was drawing a bath, a rush of water coming out of a faucet at full speed. But it wasn't close to us at all. The sound made me open my eyes, and when I did, I regretted it immediately. As clear as day, I saw a wall of water to my left coming from North Dakota. But this wall wasn't the dark shadow you usually see; this was white, just like water rushing out of a faucet.

My heart started pounding.

"Eve, focus," said Guinevere when she noticed I broke my concentration.

I shook my head and closed my eyes again, taking a deep breath of the rain-filled air surrounding us. I dug my claws into the earth to give myself a little more support and situated myself firmly on my hind legs. With all my energy focusing on lifting this landmass, my whole body began to tremble. It felt like minutes had passed, and I must've been holding my breath because I started getting dizzy. I lost focus when I opened my eyes again, feeling half defeated.

"Breathe, Eve!" yelled Oliver.

I took a deep breath and tried again. This time I didn't think about it too hard. When Guin threw that giant boulder at me, I wasn't even looking at her. My body reacted instantly to protect myself and my friends – did I just call them friends?

That's it! I thought.

All I had to do was think about saving my friends and family. If I focus on them, maybe I can pull this off. So, I did. I focused all of my energy on the safety of the ones I loved most. Thinking about their future and the lives they still have left to live. Thinking about all the fun times we have had and will have in our future because I will save them.

My heart started pounding again, and my body was warm, despite the cold shift in the air. Keeping my eyes closed, I kept concentrating on my loved ones that lived within this Region's boundaries. The air was picking up as the rain made its way closer to our location; it was moving faster than I've ever seen in my life. I couldn't believe it was already halfway across the Midwest. When the rain finally reached us, we were safe and dry within the protection spell Guinevere put around us. It allowed me to maintain my focus.

Memories started flashing through my mind of a life I never lived. I was running free as the red wolf with my pack, jumping, and playing with other wolves alike. We were all so happy, and it made my heart flutter.

The warmth in my body grew as the pleasant memories continued to surface. I felt a smile creep onto my face and moisture in my fur coming from the tears streaming down my face when the ground beneath me began shaking.

Scared of breaking my concentration, I kept my eyes closed. We were far enough away from the border itself that when the ground lifted, we stayed put.

"It's working," I heard Pepper whisper.

My eyes remained closed.

I could hear the earth breaking with every breath I took. Pieces of rock and debris from the now broken bridges fell all around us. It took every ounce of will power to keep my eyes shut. I wanted to see what I was doing.

Then I felt a hand on my shoulder.

I kept my head down and glanced out of the corner of my eye to see who approached me. It was Oli.

"Eve, look up."

When I did, my heart stopped beating. Right before my eyes was a wall of earth. I lifted the Midwest. I still couldn't believe I was capable of such a feat. As quickly as the storm began, it was over. The moment seemed to pass quicker than I anticipated, but there was evidence of the new day starting when I looked towards the sky. With the feeling of joy within me, I slowly lowered the Midwest back into place when Guinevere indicated it was safe.

Before I could process everything, the rest of the group transformed into their respective animal forms – Oliver in his beautiful black coat with white specks. Pepper had a lovely shade of green on his feathers. It was like a rainforest on a bird. In his human form, the blue hair became blue feathers on the top of his head and surrounded his eyes. That little girl that lives behind me would be proud to call him her pet bird.

And Felix.

Is it wrong to have a crush on a pet cat?

I guess if you're a human, it is, so the right question would be, is it wrong to have a crush on a cat when you're a wolf?

Felix's fur was a gorgeous shade of orange. It was more vibrant than a typical orange tabby, and the stripes were darker. His coat was longer than a medium length and looked soft. My wolf instincts made me want to rub against him to feel his fur, but my human ones said that would be creepy, and I kept to myself.

You know we can hear your thoughts, right?

Who said that?

Me, Felix, the one you're crushing on.

Whoa, Eve likes Felix?!

Ok, that was definitely Pepper. So, what you're saying is—

We can hear each other's thoughts when in animal form.

Good to know. Where's Guin?

"I'm still in human form," Guin said, and we all looked towards her.

Why don't you shift into your bee form? I thought.

"Because I can communicate in human or bee form, and I prefer this seductive body over my clumpy bee shape."

Fair point.

"Now, if you kids are satisfied with what transpired today, I will be on my way. I have other business to attend to and shall not be late."

Other business that's more important than discussing what the fuck just happened?!

"Yes, Eve. Believe it or not, tonight's near apocalypse is not the only disaster I am trying to prevent."

With that, Guinevere left in a puff of smoke. No joke. She just went *poof* and disappeared. The rest of us stood there starring at each other, well, until Pep decided it was too quiet.

Let's go for a fly! Or run, I guess! Both!

Can we just relish this moment for a minute? Felix asked

I concur; I am wondering what's next? What do we do now?

We enjoy being alive for as long as we can. Oli sounded relieved and worried, but he nuzzled his tiny head against my massive paw when he approached me. For Oli, that means he is worry-free, happy, and ready to have some fun.

Does enjoying being alive mean I get to run?

I suppose if running is what you want to do. Felix didn't sound thrilled, but I think he knew my inner wolf was itching to take full advantage of being alive.

It is. At that last thought, I howled at the waning gibbous moon that was nearly hidden now and took in a deep breath.

The remnants of the storm lingered in the air as I watched the sunrise above the horizon. The sky finished changing from the dark, overcast sky to a baby blue one streaked with pink and orange colors. The misty clouds brushed the edges of the earth when we all took off towards the sunrise. It was strange to think that it only took a night to release my magic and save a region of the United States.

But something inside was telling me that this was just the beginning.

Elle C is the author of the new novel, *Destructively Alive,* book one of the *Trial by Embers* series. She lives in St. Louis, Missouri with her boyfriend and their three fur babies, Pandora, Cozy and Toothless. In her free time, Elle enjoys watching crime shows, especially Law and Order: SVU, as well as *Dexter*, her inspiration for her new novel. For more of Elle's work, visit her website, www.ellewriting.com.